by Avery Slier

illustrated by Morgan, Inc.

HAPPY HOUSE BOOKS
Random House, Inc.

Bumpety-bump, bumpety-bump. Adam and Teddy Beddy Bear were going to the park to play. Adam pedaled his tricycle. Teddy Beddy rode in the little red wagon that Adam had tied behind it. The ride was so bouncy that Teddy Beddy had to hold on to the sides of the wagon very tightly so he wouldn't fall out.

Teddy Beddy had never been to the park before.
There were so many exciting things to do!
They swung on the swings . . .

slid down the slide . . .

and climbed on the jungle gym.

Soon Teddy Beddy was all tired out.

"Time to leave!" said Adam's mother.

Adam helped Teddy Beddy get into the wagon. Then they started for home.

Bumpety-bump, bumpety-bump. Adam pedaled down the sidewalk as fast as he could. Teddy Beddy bounced from one side of the wagon to the other. What fun he was having! Suddenly . . .

Bump! The wagon hit a crack in the sidewalk. Teddy Beddy flew through the air.

Thump! Teddy Beddy landed on the hard sidewalk.

Teddy Beddy sat up and saw Adam in the distance.
"Hey, wait for me!" Teddy Beddy called.
But Adam didn't hear him and disappeared around the corner.

Teddy Beddy raced to the end of the street and looked around. Nothing looked right. None of the houses looked like his house. None of the front yards looked like his front yard. Worst of all, none of the little boys looked like Adam.

Poor Teddy Beddy Bear! He was all alone and didn't know
what to do. So he sat down and cried.

"Well, well," said a voice. "What have we here?"

Teddy Beddy looked up and saw a police officer. "Someone must be looking for you," said the police officer. "I'd better take you home. I wonder where you live?"

Teddy Beddy didn't know what to say. When Adam went out, his mother always put a note in his pocket with his name and address on it, in case he got lost. But she had never thought to pin a note to Teddy Beddy's nightshirt. He started crying even harder.

"You look like a brave bear," said the police officer. "I'll take you back to the station house with me. We'll get you safely home." He lifted Teddy Beddy and set him on his shoulder. Together the two went off to the police station.

Bumpety-bump, bumpety-bump. Adam rode his tricycle into his front yard. Then he climbed off and walked around to the little red wagon. "Come on, Teddy Beddy," he said. "Let's go inside."

But Teddy Beddy wasn't in the wagon.

Adam ran to the sidewalk. "Teddy Beddy Bear!" he called. "Where are you?" There was no answer.

Adam's mother heard him calling to Teddy Beddy. She and Adam went to the corner of the block. Teddy Beddy was not there. They ran all the way back to the park. But Teddy Beddy was nowhere to be seen.

Without Teddy Beddy Bear, dinner that night was no fun at all. Adam pushed his green beans around the plate and spilled his milk. He didn't even eat his dessert. Apple pie didn't taste good without Teddy Beddy there for company.

"I have an idea," Adam's mother said after dinner. She called the police station and let Adam talk to the police officer who answered.

"Have you found a bear?" Adam asked. "His name is Teddy Beddy and I miss him very much." They had! They had found a bear! That afternoon another police officer had brought one into the station. But someone would have to come down and pick the bear up.

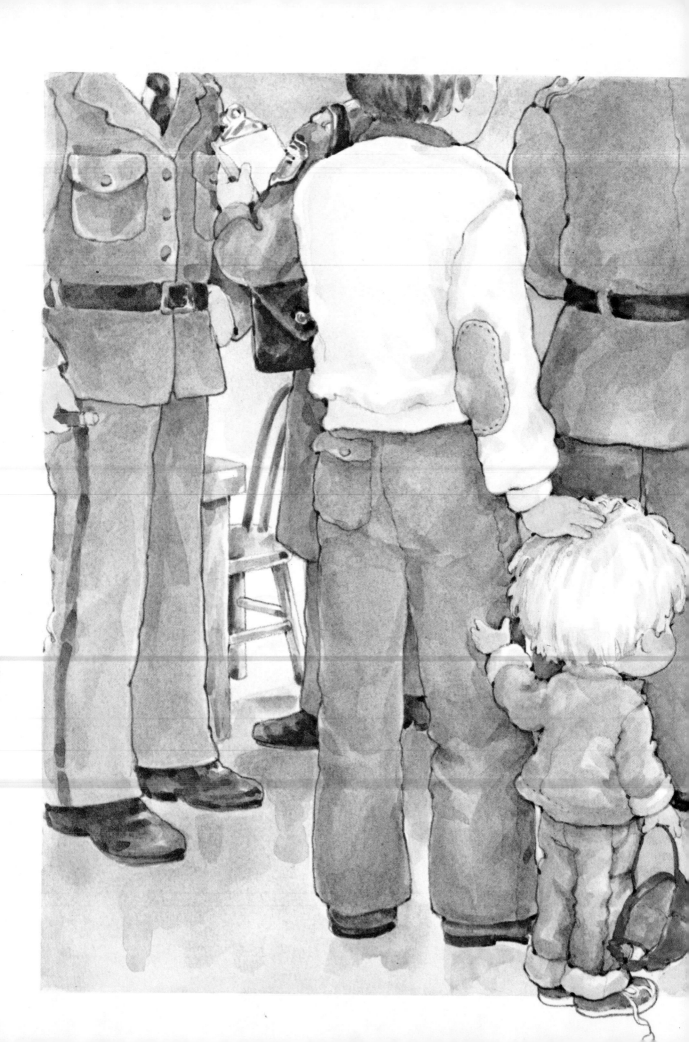

Adam and his father went to the police station. It was so crowded! Adam was afraid that he would never find Teddy Beddy.

Adam looked and looked for Teddy Beddy's face. Then, far off on the other side of the room, he saw something familiar. There on the sergeant's desk sat Teddy Beddy Bear!

"Oh, Teddy Beddy! I was afraid you'd be lost forever!" said Adam. The sergeant helped Teddy Beddy down from the desk.

The two friends hugged each other. "From now on, Teddy Beddy," said Adam, "both of us will carry our address. That way neither of us will ever get lost again." And Teddy Beddy Bear agreed!